Old Granny Fox

Thornton W. Burgess

HAWK PRESS

Published by

Hawk Press
4836/24, Ansari Road, Daryaganj
New Delhi – 110 002
Phones : 9643330713, +91-11-23278618, +91-11-35676207
E-mail: thehawkpress@gmail.com
www.thehawkpress.com

ISBN : 978-93-92322-42-6

Contents

CHAPTER I

Reddy Fox Brings Granny News

Pray who is there who would refuse

To bearer be of happy news?

—Old Granny Fox.

Snow covered the Green Meadows and the Green Forest, and ice bound the Smiling Pool and the Laughing Brook. Reddy and Granny Fox were hungry most of the time. It was not easy to find enough to eat these days, and so they spent nearly every minute they were awake in hunting. Sometimes they hunted together, but usually one went one way, and the other went another way so as to have a greater chance of finding something. If either found enough for two, the one finding it took the food back to their home if it could be carried. If not, the other was told where to find it.

For several days they had had very little indeed to eat, and they were so hungry that they were willing to take almost any chance to get a good meal. For two nights they had visited Farmer Brown's henhouse, hoping that they would be able to find a way inside. But the biddies had been securely locked up, and try as they would, they couldn't find a way in.

"It's of no use," said Granny, as they started back home after the second try, "to hope to get one of those hens at night. If we are going to get any at all, we will have to do it in broad daylight. It can be done, for I have done it before, but I don't like the idea. We are likely to be seen, and that means that Bowser the Hound will be set to hunting us."

"Pooh!" exclaimed Reddy. "What of it? It's easy enough to fool him."

"You think so, do you?" snapped Granny. "I never yet saw a young Fox who didn't think he knew all there is to know, and you're just like the rest. When you've lived as long as I have you will have learned not to be quite so sure of your own opinions. I grant you that when there is no snow on the ground, any Fox with a reasonable amount of Fox sense in his head can fool Bowser, but with snow everywhere it is a very different matter. If Bowser once takes it into his head to follow your trail these days, you will have to be smarter than I think you are to fool him. The only way you will be able to get away from him will be by going into a hole in the ground, and when you do that you will have given away a secret that will mean we will never have any peace at all. We will never know when Farmer Brown's boy will take it into his head to smoke us out. I've seen it done. No, Sir, we are not going to try for one of those hens in the daytime unless we are starving."

"I'm starving now," whined Reddy.

"No such thing!" Granny snapped. "I've been without food longer than this many a time. Have you been over to the Big River lately?"

"No," replied Reddy. "What's the use? It's frozen over. There isn't anything there."

"Perhaps not," replied Granny, "but I learned a long time ago that it is a poor plan to overlook any chance. There is a place in the Big River which never freezes because the water runs too swiftly to freeze, and I've found more than one meal washed ashore there. You go over there now while I see what I can find in the Green Forest. If neither of us finds anything, it will be time enough to think about Farmer Brown's hens to-morrow."

Much against his will Reddy obeyed. "It isn't the least bit of use," he grumbled, as he trotted towards the Big River. "There won't be anything there. It is just a waste of time."

Late that afternoon he came hurrying back, and Granny knew by the way that he cocked his ears and carried his tail that he had news of some kind. "Well, what is it?" she demanded.

"I found a dead fish that had been washed ashore," replied Reddy. "It wasn't big enough for two, so I ate it."

"Anything else?" asked Granny.

"No-o," replied Reddy slowly; "that is, nothing that will do us any good. Quacker the Wild Duck was swimming about out in the open water, but though I watched and watched he never once came ashore."

"Ha!" exclaimed Granny. "That is good news. I think we'll go Duck hunting."

CHAPTER II

Granny And Reddy Fox Go Hunting

When you're in doubt what course is right,

The thing to do is just sit tight.

—Old Granny Fox.

Jolly, round, bright Mr. Sun had just got well started on his daily climb up in the blue, blue sky that morning when he spied two figures trotting across the snow-covered Green Meadows, one behind the other. They were trotting along quite as if they had made up their minds just where they were going. They had. You see they were Granny and Reddy Fox, and they were bound for the Big River at the place where the water ran too swiftly to freeze. The day before Reddy had discovered Quacker the Wild Duck swimming about there, and now they were on their way to try to catch him.

Granny led the way and Reddy meekly followed her. To tell the truth, Reddy hadn't the least idea that they would have a chance to catch Quacker, because Quacker kept out in the water where he was as safe from them as if they were a thousand miles away. The only reason that Reddy had willingly started with Granny was the hope that he might find a dead fish washed up on the shore as he had the day before.

"Granny certainly is growing foolish in her old age," thought Reddy, as he trotted along behind her. "I told her that Quacker never once came ashore all the time I watched yesterday. I don't believe he ever comes ashore, and if she knows anything at all she ought to know that she can't catch him out there in the water. Granny used to be smart enough when she was young, I guess, but she certainly is losing her mind now. It's a pity, a great pity. I can just imagine how Quacker will laugh at her. I have to laugh myself."

He did laugh, but you may be sure he took great pains that Granny should not see him laughing. Whenever she looked around he was as sober as could be. In fact, he appeared to be quite as eager as if he felt sure they would catch Quacker. Now old Granny Fox is very wise in the ways of the Great World, and if Reddy could have known what was going on in her mind as she led the way to the Big River, he might not have felt quite so sure of his own smartness. Granny was doing some quiet laughing herself.

"He thinks I'm old and foolish and don't know what I'm about, the young scamp!" thought she. "He thinks he has learned all there is to learn. It isn't the least use in the world to try to tell him anything. When young folks feel the way he does, it is a waste of time to talk to them. He has got to be shown. There is nothing like experience to take the conceit out of these youngsters."

Now conceit is the feeling that you know more than any one else. Perhaps you do. Then again, perhaps you don't. So sometimes it is best not to be too sure of your own opinion. Reddy was sure. He trotted along behind old Granny Fox and planned smart things to say to her when she found that there wasn't a chance to catch Quacker the Duck. I am afraid, very much afraid, that Reddy was planning to be saucy. People who think themselves smart are quite apt to be saucy.

Presently they came to the bank of the Big River. Old Granny Fox told Reddy to sit still while she crept up behind some bushes where she could peek out over the Big River. He grinned as he watched her. He was still grinning when she tiptoed back. He expected to see her face long with disappointment. Instead she looked very much pleased.

"Quacker is there," said she, "and I think he will make us a very good dinner. Creep up behind those bushes and see for yourself, then come back here and tell me what you think we'd better do to get him."

So Reddy stole up behind the bushes, and this time it was Granny who grinned as she watched. As he crept along, Reddy wondered if it could be that for once Quacker had come ashore. Granny seemed so sure they could catch him that this must be the case. But when he peeped through the hushes, there was Quacker way out in the middle of the open water just where he had been the day before.

CHAPTER III

Reddy Is Sure Granny Has Lost Her Senses

Perhaps 'tis just as well that we

Can't see ourselves as others see.

—Old Granny Fox.

"Just as I thought," muttered Reddy Fox as he peeped through the bushes on the bank of the Big River and saw Quacker swimming about in the water where it ran too swiftly to freeze. "We've got just as much chance of catching him as I have of jumping over the moon. That's what I'll tell Granny."

He crept back carefully so as not to be seen by Quacker, and when he had reached the place where Granny was waiting for him, his face wore a very impudent look.

"Well," said Granny Fox, "what shall we do to catch him?"

"Learn to swim like a fish and fly like a bird," replied Reddy in such a saucy tone that Granny had hard work to keep from boxing his ears.

"You mean that you think he can't be caught?" said she quietly.

"I don't think anything about it; I know he can't!" snapped Reddy. "Not by us, anyway," he added.

"I suppose you wouldn't even try?" retorted Granny.

"I'm old enough to know when I'm wasting my time," replied Reddy with a toss of his head.

"In other words you think I'm a silly old Fox who has lost her senses," said Granny sharply.

"No-o. I didn't say that," protested Reddy, looking very uncomfortable.

"But you think it," declared Granny. "Now look here, Mr. Smarty, you do just as I tell you. You creep back there where you can watch Quacker and all that happens, and mind that you keep out of his sight.

Now go."

Reddy went. There was nothing else to do. He didn't dare disobey. Granny watched until Reddy had readied his hiding-place. Then what do you think she did? Why, she walked right out on the little beach just below Reddy and in plain sight of Quacker! Yes, Sir, that is what she did!

Then began such a queer performance that it is no wonder that Reddy was sure Granny had lost her senses. She rolled over and over. She chased her tail round and round until it made Reddy dizzy to watch her. She jumped up in the air. She raced back and forth. She played with a bit of stick. And all the time she didn't pay the least attention to Quacker the Duck.

Reddy stared and stared. Whatever had come over Granny? She was crazy. Yes, Sir, that must be the matter. It must be that she had gone without food so long that she had gone crazy. Poor Granny! She was in her second childhood. Reddy could remember how he had done such things when he was very young, just by way of showing how fine he felt. But for a grown-up Fox to do such things was undignified, to say the least. You know Reddy thinks a great deal of dignity. It was worse than undignified; it was positively disgraceful. He did hope that none of his neighbors would happen along and see Granny cutting up so. He never would hear the end of it if they did.

Over and over rolled Granny, and around and around she chased her tail. The snow flew up in a cloud. And all the time she made no sound. Reddy was just trying to decide whether to go off and leave her until she had regained her common sense, or to go out and try to stop her, when he happened to look out in the open water where Quacker was. Quacker was sitting up as straight as he could. In fact, he had his wings raised to help him sit up on his tail, the better to see what old Granny Fox was doing.

"As I live," muttered Reddy, "I believe that fellow is nearer than he was!"

Reddy crouched lower than ever, and instead of watching Granny he watched Quacker the Duck.

CHAPTER IV

Quacker The Duck Grows Curious

The most curious thing in the world is curiosity.

—Old Granny Fox.

Old Granny Fox never said a truer thing than that. It is curious, very curious, how sometimes curiosity will get the best of even the wisest and most sensible of people. Even Old Granny Fox herself has been known to be led into trouble by it. We expect it of Peter Rabbit, but Peter isn't a bit more curious than some others of whom we do not expect it.

Now Quacker the Wild Duck is the last one in the world you would expect to be led into trouble by curiosity. Quacker had spent the summer in the Far North with Honker the Goose. In fact, he had been born there. He had started for the far away Southland at the same time Honker had, but when he reached the Big River he had found plenty to eat and had decided to stay until he had to move on. The Big River had frozen over everywhere except in this one place where the water was too swift to freeze, and there Quacker had remained. You see, he was a good diver and on the bottom of the river he found plenty to eat. No one could get at him out there, unless it were Roughleg the Hawk, and if Roughleg did happen along, all he had to do was to dive and come up far away to laugh and make fun of Roughleg. The water couldn't get through his oily feathers, and so he didn't mind how cold it was.

Now in his home in the Far North there were so many dangers that Quacker had early learned to be always on the watch and to take the best of care of himself. On his way down to the Big River he had been hunted by men with terrible guns, and he had learned all about them. In fact, he felt quite able to keep out of harm's way. He rather prided himself that there was no one smart enough to catch him.

I suspect he thought he knew all there was to know. In this respect he was a good deal like Reddy Fox himself. That was because he was young. It is the way with young Ducks and Foxes and with some other youngsters I know.

When Quacker first saw Granny Fox on the little beach, he flirted his absurd little tail and smiled as he thought how she must wish she could catch him. But so far as he could see, Granny didn't once look at him.

"She doesn't know I'm out here at all," thought Quacker. Then suddenly he sat up very straight and looked with all his might. What under the sun was the matter with that Fox? She was acting as if she had suddenly lost her senses.

Over and over she rolled. Around and around she spun. She turned somersaults. She lay on her back and kicked her heels in the air. Never in his life had he known any one to act like that. There must be something the matter with her.

Quacker began to get excited. He couldn't keep his eyes off Old Granny Fox. He began to swim nearer. He wanted to see better. He quite forgot she was a Fox. She moved so fast that she was just a queer red spot on the beach. Whatever she was doing was very curious and very exciting. He swam nearer and nearer. The excitement was catching. He began to swim in circles himself. All the time he drew nearer and nearer to the shore. He didn't have the least bit of fear. He was just curious. He wanted to see better.

All the time Granny was cutting up her antics, she was watching Quacker, though he didn't suspect it. As he swam nearer and nearer to the shore, Granny rolled and tumbled farther and farther back. At last Quacker was close to the shore. If he kept on, he would be right on the land in a few minutes. And all the time he stared and stared. No thought of danger entered his head. You see, there was no room because it was so filled with curiosity.

"In a minute more I'll have him," thought Granny, and whirled faster than ever. And just then something happened.

CHAPTER V

Reddy Fox Is Afraid To Go Home

Yes, Sir, a chicken track is good to see, but
it often puts nothing but water in my mouth.
—Old Granny Fox.

Reddy Fox thought of that saying many times as he hunted through the Green Forest that night, afraid to go home. You see, he had almost dined on Quacker the Duck over at the Big River that day and then hadn't, and it was all his own fault. That was why he was afraid to go home. From his hiding-place on the bank he had watched Quacker swim in and in until he was almost on the shore where old Granny Fox was whirling and rolling and tumbling about as if she had entirely lost her senses. Indeed, Reddy had been quite sure that she had when she began. It wasn't until he saw that curiosity was drawing Quacker right in so that in a minute or two Granny would be able to catch him, that he understood that Granny was anything but crazy, and really was teaching him a new trick as well as trying to catch a dinner.

When he realized this, he should have been ashamed of himself for doubting the smartness of Granny and for thinking that he knew all there was to know. But he was too much excited for any such thoughts. Nearer and nearer to the shore came Quacker, his eyes fixed on the red, whirling form of Granny. Reddy's own eyes gleamed with excitement. Would Quacker keep on right up to the shore? Nearer and nearer and nearer he came. Reddy squirmed uneasily. He couldn't see as well as he wanted to. The bushes behind which he was lying were in his way. He wanted to see Granny make that jump which would mean a dinner for both.

Forgetting what Granny had charged him, Reddy eagerly raised his head to look over the edge of the bank. Now it just happened that at that very minute Quacker chanced to look that way. His quick eyes caught the movement of Reddy's head and in an instant all his curiosity vanished. That sharp face peering at him over the edge of the bank could mean but one thing—danger! It was all a trick! He saw through it now. Like a flash he turned. There was the whistle of stiff wings beating the air and the patter of feet striking the water as he got under way. Then he flew out to the safety of the open water. Granny sprang, but she was just too late and succeeded in doing no more than wet her feet.

Of course, Granny didn't know what had frightened Quacker, not at first, anyway. But she had her suspicions. She turned and looked up at the place where Reddy had been hiding. She couldn't see him. Then she bounded up the bank. There was no Reddy there, but far away across the snow-covered Green Meadows was a red spot growing smaller and smaller. Reddy was running away. Then she knew. At first Granny was very angry. You know it is a dreadful thing to be hungry and have a good dinner disappear just as it is almost within reach.

"I'll teach that young scamp a lesson he won't soon forget when I get home," she muttered, as she watched him. Then she went back to the edge of the Big River and there she found a dead fish which had been washed ashore. It was a very good fish, and when she had eaten it Granny felt better.

"Anyway," thought she, "I have taught him a new trick and one he is n't likely to forget. He knows now that Granny still knows a few tricks that he doesn't, and next time he won't feel so sure he knows it all. I guess it was worth while even if I didn't catch Quacker. My, but he would have tasted good!" Granny smacked her lips and started for home.

But Reddy, with a guilty conscience, was afraid to go home. And so, miserable and hungry, he hunted through the Green Forest all the long night and wished and wished that he had heeded what old Granny Fox had told him.

CHAPTER VI

Old Granny Fox Is Caught Napping

The wisest folks will make mistakes, but

if they are truly wise they will profit from them.

—Old Granny Fox.

There is a saying among the little people of the Green Forest and the Green Meadows which runs something like this:

"You must your eyes wide open keep

To catch Old Granny Fox asleep."

Of course this means that Old Granny Fox is so smart, so clever, so keenly on the watch at all times, that he must be very smart indeed who fools her or gets ahead of her. Reddy Fox is smart, very smart. But Reddy isn't nearly as smart as Old Granny Fox. You see, he hasn't lived nearly as long, so of course there is much knowledge of many things stored away in Granny's head of which Reddy knows little.

But once in a while even the smartest people are caught napping. Yes, Sir, that does happen. They will be careless sometimes. It was just so with Old Granny Fox. With all her smartness and cleverness and wisdom she grew careless, and all the smartness and cleverness and wisdom in the world is useless if the possessor becomes careless.

You see, Old Granny Fox had become so used to thinking that she was smarter than any one else, unless it was Old Man Coyote, that she actually believed that no one was smart enough ever to surprise her. Yes, Sir, she actually believed that. Now, you know when a person reaches the point of thinking that no one else in all the Great World is quite so smart, that person is like Peter Rabbit when he made ready one winter day to jump out on the smooth ice of the Smiling Pool,—getting ready for a fall. It was this way with Old Granny Fox.

Because she had lived near Farmer Brown's so long and had been hunted so often by Farmer Brown's boy and by Bowser the Hound, she had got the idea in her head that no matter what she did they would not be able to catch her. So at last she grew careless. Yes, Sir, she grew careless. And that is something no Fox or anybody else can afford to do.

Now on the edge of the Green Forest was a warm, sunny knoll, which, as you know, is a sort of little hill. It overlooked the Green Meadows and was quite the most pleasant and comfortable place for a sun-nap that ever was. At least, that is what Old Granny Fox thought. She took sun-naps there very often. It was her favorite resting place. When Bowser the Hound had found her trail and had chased her until she was tired of running and had had quite all the exercise she needed or wanted, she would play one of her clever tricks by which to make Bowser lose her trail. Then she would hurry straight to that knoll to rest and grin at her own smartness.

It happened that she did this one day when there was fresh snow on the ground. Of course, every time she put a foot down she left a print in the snow. And where she curled up in the sun she left the print of her body. They were very plain to see, were these prints, and Farmer Brown's boy saw them.

He had been tramping through the Green Forest late in the afternoon and just by chance happened across Granny's footprints. Just for fun he followed them and so came to the sunny knoll. Granny had left some time before, but of course she couldn't take the print of her body with her. That remained in the snow, and Farmer Brown's boy saw it and knew instantly what it meant. He grinned, and could Granny Fox have seen that grin, she would have been uncomfortable. You see, he knew that he had found the place where Granny was in the habit of taking a sun-nap.

"So," said he, "this is the place where you rest, Old Mrs. Fox, after running Bowser almost off his feet. I think we will give you a surprise one of these days. Yes, indeed, I think we will give you a surprise. You have fooled us many times, and now it is our turn."

The next day Farmer Brown's boy shouldered his terrible gun and sent Bowser the Hound to hunt for the trail of Old Granny Fox. It wasn't long before Bowser's great voice told all the Great World that he had found Granny's tracks. Farmer Brown's boy grinned just as he had the day before. Then with his terrible gun he went over to the Green

Forest and hid under some pine boughs right on the edge of that sunny knoll.

He waited patiently a long, long time. He heard Bowser's great voice growing more and more excited as he followed Old Granny Fox. By and by Bowser stopped baying and began to yelp impatiently. Farmer Brown's boy knew exactly what that meant. It meant that Granny had played one of her smart tricks and Bowser had lost her trail.

A few minutes later out of the Green Forest came Old Granny Fox, and she was grinning, for once more she had fooled Bowser the Hound and now could take a nap in peace. Still grinning, she turned around two or three times to make herself comfortable and then, with a sigh of contentment, curled up for a sun-nap, and in a few minutes was asleep. And just a little way off behind the pine boughs sat Farmer Brown's boy holding his terrible gun and grinning. At last he had caught Old Granny Fox napping.

CHAPTER VII

Granny Fox Has A Bad Dream

Nothing ever simply happens;
Bear that point in mind.
If you look long and hard enough
A cause you'll always find.
—Old Granny Fox.

Old Granny Fox was dreaming. Yes, Sir, she was dreaming. There she lay, curled up on the sunny little knoll on the edge of the Green Forest, fast asleep and dreaming. It was a very pleasant and very comfortable place indeed. You see, jolly, round, bright Mr. Sun poured his warmest rays right down there from the blue, blue sky. When Old Granny Fox was tired, she often slipped over there for a short nap and sun-bath even in winter. She was quite sure that no one knew anything about it. It was one of her secrets.

This morning Old Granny Fox was very tired, unusually so. In the first place she had been out hunting all night. Then, before she could reach home, Bowser the Hound had found her tracks and started to follow them. Of course, it wouldn't have done to go home then. It wouldn't have done at all. Bowser would have followed her straight there and so found out where she lived. So she had led Bowser far away across the Green Meadows and through the Green Forest and finally played one of her smart tricks which had so mixed her tracks that Bowser could no longer follow them. While he had sniffed and snuffed and snuffed and sniffed with that wonderful nose of his, trying to find out where she had gone, Old Granny Fox had trotted straight to the sunny knoll and there curled up to rest. Right away she fell asleep.

Now Old Granny Fox, like most of the other little people of the Green Forest and the Green Meadows, sleeps with her ears wide open. Her eyes may be closed, but not her ears. Those are always on guard, even when she is asleep, and at the least sound open fly her eyes, and she is ready to run. If it were not for the way her sharp ears keep guard, she wouldn't dare take naps in the open right in broad daylight. If you ever want to catch a Fox asleep, you mustn't make the teeniest, weeniest noise. Just remember that.

Now Old Granny Fox had no sooner closed her eyes than she began to dream. At first it was a very pleasant dream, the pleasantest dream a Fox can have. It was of a chicken dinner, all the chicken she could eat. Granny certainly enjoyed that dream. It made her smack her lips quite as if it were a real and not a dream dinner she was enjoying.

But presently the dream changed and became a bad dream. Yes, indeed, it became a bad dream. It was as bad as at first it had been good. It seemed to Granny that Bowser the Hound had become very smart, smarter than she had ever known him to be before. Do what she would, she couldn't fool him. Not one of all the tricks she knew, and she knew a great many, fooled him at all. They didn't puzzle him long enough for her to get her breath.

Bowser kept getting nearer and nearer and nearer, all in the dream, you know, until it seemed as if his great voice sounded right at her very heels. She was so tired that it seemed to her that she couldn't run another step. It was a very, very real dream. You know dreams sometimes do seem very real indeed. This was the way it was with the bad dream of Old Granny Fox. It seemed to her that she could feel the breath of Bowser the Hound and that his great jaws were just going to close on her and shake her to death.

"Oh! Oh!" cried Granny and waked herself up. Her eyes flew open. Then she gave a great sigh of relief as she realized that her terrible fright was only a bad dream and that she was curled up right on the dear, familiar, old, sunny knoll and not running for her life at all.

Old Granny Fox smiled to think what a fright she had had and then,—well, she didn't know whether she was really awake or still dreaming! No, Sir, she didn't. For a full minute she couldn't be sure whether what she saw was real or part of that dreadful dream. You see, she was staring into the face of Farmer Brown's boy and the muzzle of his dreadful gun!

For just a few seconds she didn't move. She couldn't. She was too frightened to move. Then she knew what she saw was real and not a dream at all. There wasn't the least bit of doubt about it. That was Farmer Brown's boy, and that was his dreadful gun! All in a flash she knew that Farmer Brown's boy must have been hiding behind those pine boughs.

Poor Old Granny Fox! For once in her life she had been caught napping. She hadn't the least hope in the world. Farmer Brown's boy had only to fire that dreadful gun, and that would be the end of her. She knew it.

CHAPTER VIII

What Farmer Brown's Boy Did

In time of danger heed this rule:

Think hard and fast, but pray keep cool.

—Old Granny Fox.

Poor Old Granny Fox! She had thought that she had been in tight places before, but never, never had she been in such a tight place as this. There stood Farmer Brown's boy looking along the barrel of his dreadful gun straight at her, and only such a short distance, such a very short distance away! It wasn't the least bit of use to run. Granny knew that. That dreadful gun would go "bang!" and that would be the end of her.

For a few seconds she stared at Farmer Brown's boy, too frightened to move or even think. Then she began to wonder why that dreadful gun didn't go off. What was Farmer Brown's boy waiting for? She got to her feet. She was sure that the first step would be her last, yet she couldn't stay there.

How could Fanner Brown's boy do such a dreadful thing? Somehow, his freckled face didn't look cruel. He was even beginning to grin. That must be because he had caught her napping and knew that this time she couldn't possibly get away from him as she had so many times before. "Oh!" sobbed Old Granny Fox under her breath.

And right at that very instant Farmer Brown's boy did something. What do you think it was? No, he didn't shoot her. He didn't fire his dreadful gun. What do you think he did do? Why, he threw a snowball at Old Granny Fox and shouted "Boo!" That is what he did and all he did, except to laugh as Granny gave a great leap and then made those black legs of hers fly as never before.

Every instant Granny expected to hear that dreadful gun, and it seemed as if her heart would burst with fright as she ran, thinking each jump would be the last one. But the dreadful gun didn't bang, and after a little, when she felt she was safe, she turned to look back over her shoulder. Farmer Brown's boy was standing right where she had last seen him, and he was laughing harder than ever. Yes, Sir, he was laughing, and though Old Granny Fox didn't think so at the time, his laugh was good to hear, for it was good-natured and merry and all that an honest laugh should be.

"Go it, Granny! Go it!" shouted Farmer Brown's boy. "And the next time you are tempted to steal my chickens, just remember that I caught you napping and let you off when I might have shot you. Just remember that and leave my chickens alone."

Now it happened that Tommy Tit the Chickadee had seen all that had happened, and he fairly bubbled over with joy. "Dee, dee, dee, Chickadee! It is just as I have always said—Farmer Brown's boy isn't bad. He'd be friends with every one if every one would let him," he cried.

"Maybe, maybe," grumbled Sammy Jay, who also had seen all that had happened. "But he's altogether too smart for me to trust. Oh, my! oh, my! What news this will be to tell! Old Granny Fox will never hear the end of it. If ever again she boasts of how smart she is, all we will have to do will be to remind her of the time Farmer Brown's boy caught her napping. Ho! ho! ho! I must hurry along and find my cousin, Blacky the Crow. This will tickle him half to death."

As for Old Granny Fox, she feared Farmer Brown's boy more than ever, not because of what he had done to her but because of what he had not done. You see, nothing could make her believe that he wanted to be her friend. She thought he had let her get away just to show her that he was smarter than she. Instead of thankfulness, hate and fear filled Granny's heart. You know—

People who themselves do ill

For others seldom have good will.

CHAPTER IX

Reddy Fox Hears About Granny Fox

Though you may think another wrong
And be quite positive you're right,
Don't let your temper get away;
And try at least to be polite.
—Old Granny Fox.

Sammy Jay hurried through the Green Forest, chuckling as he flew. Sammy was brimming over with the news he had to tell,—how Old Granny Fox had been caught napping by Farmer Brown's boy. Sammy wouldn't have believed it if any one had told him. No, Sir, he wouldn't. But he had seen it with his own eyes, and it tickled him almost to pieces to think that Old Granny Fox, whom everybody thought so sly and clever and smart, had been caught actually asleep by the very one of whom she was most afraid, but at whom she always had turned up her nose.

Presently Sammy spied Reddy Fox trotting along the Lone Little Path. Reddy was forever boasting of how smart Granny Fox was. He had boasted of it so much that everybody was sick of hearing him. When he saw Reddy trotting along the Lone Little Path, Sammy chuckled harder than ever. He hid in a thick hemlock-tree and as Reddy passed he shouted:

"Had I such a stupid old Granny
As some folks who think they are smart,
I never would boast of my Granny,
But live by myself quite apart!"

Reddy looked up angrily. He couldn't see Sammy Jay, but he knew Sammy's voice. There is no mistaking that. Everybody knows the voice of Sammy Jay. Of course it was foolish, very foolish of Reddy to be angry, and still more foolish to show that he was angry. Had he stopped a minute to think, he would have known that Sammy was saying such a mean, provoking thing just to make him angry, and that the angrier he became the better pleased Sammy Jay would be. But like a great many people, Reddy allowed his temper to get the better of his common sense.

"Who says Granny Fox is stupid?" he snarled.

"I do," replied Sammy Jay promptly. "I say she is stupid."

"She is smarter than anybody else in all the Green Forest and on all the Green Meadows. She is smarter than anybody else in all the Great World," boasted Reddy, and he really believed it.

"She isn't smart enough to fool Farmer Brown's boy," taunted Sammy.

"What's that? Who says so? Has anything happened to Granny Fox?" Reddy forgot his anger in a sudden great fear. Could Granny have been shot by Farmer Brown's boy?

"Nothing much, only Farmer Brown's boy caught her napping in broad daylight," replied Sammy, and chuckled so that Reddy heard him.

"I don't believe it!" snapped Reddy. "I don't believe a word of it! Nobody ever yet caught Old Granny Fox napping, and nobody ever will."

"I don't care whether you believe it or not; it's so, for I saw him," retorted Sammy Jay.

"You—you—you—" began Reddy Fox.

"Go ask Tommy Tit the Chickadee if it isn't true. He saw him too," interrupted Sammy Jay.

"Dee, dee, dee, Chickadee! It's so, and Farmer Brown's boy only threw a snowball at her and let her run away without shooting at her," declared a new voice. There sat Tommy Tit himself.

Reddy didn't know what to think or say. He just couldn't believe it, yet he had never known Tommy Tit to tell an untruth. Sammy Jay alone he wouldn't have believed. Then Tommy Tit and Sammy Jay told Reddy all about what they had seen, how Farmer Brown's boy had surprised Old Granny Fox and then allowed her to go unharmed. Reddy had to believe it. If Tommy Tit said it was so, it must be so.

Reddy Fox started off to hunt up Old Granny Fox and ask her about it. But a sudden thought popped into his red head, and he changed his mind.

"I won't say a thing about it until some time when Granny scolds me for being careless," muttered Reddy, with a sly grin. "Then I'll see what she has to say. I guess she won't scold me so much after this."

Reddy grinned more than ever, which wasn't a bit nice of him. Instead of being sorry that Old Granny Fox had had such a fright, he was planning how he would get even with her when she should scold him for his own carelessness.

CHAPTER X

Reddy Fox Is Impudent

A saucy tongue is dangerous to possess;

Be sure some day 't will get you in a mess.

—Old Granny Fox.

Reddy Fox is headstrong and, like most headstrong people, is given to thinking that his way is the best way just because it is his way. He is smart, is Reddy Fox. Yes, indeed, Reddy Fox is very, very smart. He has to be in order to live. But a great deal of what he knows he learned from Old Granny Fox. The very best tricks he knows she taught him. She began teaching him when he was so little that he tumbled over his own feet. It was she who taught him how to hunt, that it is better never to steal chickens near home but to go a long way off for them, and how to fool Bowser the Hound.

It was Granny who taught Reddy how to use his little black nose to follow the tracks of careless young Rabbits, and how to catch Meadow Mice under the snow. In fact, there is little Reddy knows which he didn't learn from wise, shrewd Old Granny Fox.

But as he grew bigger and bigger, until he was quite as big as Granny herself, he forgot what he owed to her. He grew to have a very good opinion of himself and to feel that he knew just about all there was to know. So sometimes when he had done foolish or careless things and Granny had scolded him, telling him he was big enough and old enough to know better, he would sulk and go off muttering to himself. But he never quite dared to be openly disrespectful to Granny, and this, of course, was quite as it should have been.

"If only I could catch Granny doing something foolish or careless," he would say to himself. But he never could, and he had begun to think that he never would. But now at last Granny, clever Old Granny Fox, had been careless! She had allowed Farmer Brown's boy to catch her napping! Reddy did wish he had been there to see it himself. But anyway, he had been told about it, and he made up his mind that the next time Granny said anything sharp to him about his carelessness he would have something to say back. Yes, Sir, Reddy Fox was deliberately planning to answer back, which, as you know, is always disrespectful to one's elders.

At last the chance came. Reddy did a thing no truly wise Fox ever will do. He went two nights in succession to the same henhouse, and the second time he barely escaped being shot. Old Granny Fox found out about it. How she found out Reddy doesn't know to this day, but find out she did, and she gave him such a scolding as even her sharp tongue had seldom given him.

"You are the stupidest Fox I ever heard of," scolded Granny.

"I'm no more stupid than you are!" retorted Reddy in the most impudent way.

"What's that?" demanded Granny. "What's that you said?"

"I said I'm no more stupid than you are, and what is more, I hope I'm not so stupid. I know better than to take a nap in broad daylight right under the very nose of Farmer Brown's boy." Reddy grinned in the most impudent way as he said this.

Granny's eyes snapped. Then things happened. Reddy was cuffed this way and cuffed that way and cuffed the other way until it seemed to him that the air was full of black paws, every one of which landed on his head or face with a sting that made him whimper and put his tail between his legs, and finally howl.

"There!" cried Granny, when at last she had to stop because she was quite out of breath. "Perhaps that will teach you to be respectful to your elders. I was careless and stupid, and I am perfectly ready to admit it, because it has taught me a lesson. Wisdom often is gained through mistakes, but never when one is not willing to admit the mistakes. No Fox lives long who makes the same mistake twice. And those who are impudent to their elders come to no good end. I've got a fat goose hidden away for dinner, but you will get none of it."

"I—I wish I'd never heard of Granny's mistake," whined Reddy to himself as he crept dinnerless to bed.

"You ought to wish that you hadn't been impudent," whispered a small voice down inside him.

CHAPTER XI

After The Storm

The joys and the sunshine that make us glad;
The worries and troubles that makes us sad
Must come to an end; so why complain
Of too little sun or too much rain?
—Old Granny Fox.

The thing to do is to make the most of the sunshine while it lasts, and when it rains to look forward to the corning of the sun again, knowing that conic it surely will. A dreadful storm was keeping the little people of the Green Forest, the Green Meadows, and the Old Orchard prisoners in their own homes or in such places of shelter as they had been able to find.

But it couldn't last forever, and they knew it. Knowing this was all that kept some of them alive.

You see, they were starving. Yes, Sir, they were starving. You and I would be very hungry, very hungry indeed, if we had to go without food for two whole days, but if we were snug and warm it wouldn't do us any real harm. With the little wild friends, especially the little feathered folks, it is a very different matter. You see, they are naturally so active that they have to fill their stomachs very often in order to supply their little bodies with heat and energy. So when their food supply is wholly cut off, they starve or else freeze to death in a very short time. A great many little lives are ended this way in every long, hard winter storm.

It was late in the afternoon of the second day when rough Brother North Wind decided that he had shown his strength and fierceness long enough, and rumbling and grumbling retired from the Green Meadows and the Green Forest, blowing the snow clouds away with him. For just a little while before it was time for him to go to bed behind the Purple Hills, jolly, round, red Mr. Sun smiled down on the white land,

and never was his smile more welcome. Out from their shelters hurried all the little prisoners, for they must make the most of the short time before the coming of the cold night.

Little Tommy Tit the Chickadee was so weak that he could hardly fly, and he shook with chills. He made straight for the apple-tree where Farmer Brown's boy always keeps a piece of suet tied to a branch for Tommy and his friends. Drummer the Woodpecker was there before him. Now it is one of the laws of politeness among the feathered folk that when one is eating from a piece of suet a newcomer shall await his turn.

"Dee, dee, dee!" said Tommy Tit faintly but cheerfully, for he couldn't be other than cheery if he tried. "Dee, dee, dee! That looks good to me."

"It is good," mumbled Drummer, pecking away at the suet greedily. "Come on, Tommy Tit. Don't wait for me, for I won't be through for a long time. I'm nearly starved, and I guess you must be."

"I am," confessed Tommy, as he flew over beside Drummer. "Thank you ever so much for not making me wait."

"Don't mention it," replied Drummer, with his mouth full. "This is no time for politeness. Here comes Yank Yank the Nuthatch. I guess there is room for him too."

Yank Yank was promptly invited to join them and did so after apologizing for seeming so greedy.

"If I couldn't get my stomach full before night, I certainly should freeze to death before morning," said he. "What a blessing it is to have all this good food waiting for us. If I had to hunt for my usual food on the trees, I certainly should have to give up and die. It took all my strength to get over here. My, I feel like a new bird already! Here comes Sammy Jay. I wonder if he will try to drive us away as he usually does."

Sammy did nothing of the kind. He was very meek and most polite. "Can you make room for a starving fellow to get a bite?" he asked. "I wouldn't ask it but that I couldn't last another night without food."

"Dee, dee, dee! Always room for one more," replied Tommy Tit, crowding over to give Sammy room. "Wasn't that a dreadful storm?"

"Worst I ever knew," mumbled Sammy. "I wonder if I ever will be warm again."

Until their stomachs were full, not another word was said. Meanwhile Chatterer the Red Squirrel had discovered that the storm was over. As he floundered through the snow to another apple-tree he saw Tommy Tit and his friends, and in his heart he rejoiced that they had found food waiting for them. His own troubles were at an end, for in the tree he was headed for was a store of corn.

CHAPTER XII

Granny And Reddy Fox Hunt In Vain

Old Mother Nature's plans for good

Quite often are not understood.

—Old Granny Fox.

Tommy Tit and Drummer the Woodpecker and Yank Yank the Nuthatch and Sammy Jay and Chatterer the Red Squirrel were not the only ones who were out and about as soon as the great storm ended. Oh, my, no! No, indeed! Everybody who was not sleeping the winter away, or who had not a store of food right at hand, was out. But not all were so fortunate as Tommy Tit and his friends in finding a good meal.

Peter Rabbit and Mrs. Peter came out of the hole in the heart of the dear Old Briar-patch, where they had managed to keep comfortably warm, and at once began to fill their stomachs with bark from young trees and tender tips of twigs. It was very coarse food, but it would take away that empty feeling. Mrs. Grouse burst out of the snow and hurried to get a meal before dark. She had no time to be particular, and so she ate spruce buds. They were very bitter and not much to her liking, but she was too hungry, and night was too near for her to be fussy. She was thankful to have that much.

Granny Fox and Reddy were out too. They didn't need to hurry because, as you know, they could hunt all night, but they were so hungry that they just had to be looking for something to eat. They knew, of course, that everybody else would be out, and they hoped that some of these little people would be so weak that they could easily be caught. That seems like a dreadful hope, doesn't it? But one of the first laws of Old Mother Nature is self-preservation. That means to save your own life first. So perhaps Granny and Reddy are not to be blamed for hoping that some of their neighbors might be caught easily because of the great storm. They were very hungry indeed, and they could not eat bark like Peter Rabbit, or buds like Mrs. Grouse, or seeds like Whitefoot the

Woodmouse. Their teeth and stomachs are not made for such food.

It was hard going for Granny and Reddy Fox. The snow was soft and deep in many places, and they had to keep pretty close to those places where rough Brother North Wind had blown away enough of the snow to make walking fairly easy. They soon found that their hope that they would find some of their neighbors too weak to escape was quite in vain. When jolly, round, red Mr. Sun dropped clown behind the Purple Hills to go to bed, their stomachs were quite as empty as when they had started out.

"We'll go down to the Old Briar-patch. I don't believe it will be of much use, but you never can tell until you try. Peter Rabbit may take it into his silly head to come outside," said Granny, leading the way.

When they reached the dear Old Briar-patch they found that Peter was not outside. In fact, peering between the brambles and bushes, they could see his little brown form bobbing about as he hunted for tender bark. He had already made little paths along which he could hop easily. Peter saw them almost as soon as they saw him.

"Hard times these," said Peter pleasantly. "I hope your stomachs are not as empty as mine." He pulled a strip of bark from a young tree and began to chew it. This was more than Reddy could stand. To see Peter eating while his own stomach was just one great big ache from emptiness was too much.

"I'm going in there and catch him, or drive him out where you can catch him, if I tear my coat all to pieces!" snarled Reddy.

Peter stopped chewing and sat up. "Come right along, Reddy. Come right along if you want to, but I would advise you to save your skin and your coat," said he.

Reddy's only reply was a snarl as he pushed his way under the brambles. He yelped as they tore his coat and scratched his face, but he kept on. Now Peter's paths were very cunningly made. He had cut them through the very thickest of the briars just big enough for himself and Mrs. Peter to hop along comfortably. But Reddy is so much bigger that he had to force his way through and in places crawl flat on his stomach, which was very slow work, to say nothing of the painful scratches from the briars. It was no trouble at all for Peter to keep out of his way, and before long Reddy gave up. Without a word Granny Fox led the way to the Green Forest. They would try to find where Mrs. Grouse was sleeping under the snow. But though they hunted all night, they failed to find her, for she wisely had gone to bed in a spruce-tree.

CHAPTER XIII

Granny Fox Admits Growing Old

Who will not admit he is older each day

fools no one but himself.

—Old Granny Fox.

Old Granny Fox is a spry old lady for her age. If you don't believe it just try to catch her. But spry as she is, she isn't as spry as she used to be. No, Sir, Granny Fox isn't as spry as she used to be. The truth is, Granny is getting old. She never would admit it, and Reddy never had realized it until the day after the great storm. All that night they had hunted in vain for something to eat and at daylight had crept into their house to rest awhile before starting on another hunt. They had neither the strength nor the courage to search any longer then. Wading through snow is very hard work at best and very tiresome, but when your stomach has been empty for so long that you almost begin to wonder what food tastes like, it becomes harder work still. You see, it is food that makes strength, and lack of food takes away strength.

This was why Granny and Reddy Fox just HAD to rest. Hungry as they were, they HAD to give up for awhile. Reddy flung himself down, and if ever there was a discouraged young Fox he was that one. "I wish I were dead," he moaned.

"Tut, tut, tut!" said Granny Fox sharply. "That's no way for a young Fox to talk! I'm ashamed of you. I am indeed." Then she added more kindly: "I know just how you feel. Just try to forget your empty stomach and rest awhile. We have had a tiresome, disappointing, discouraging night, but when you are rested things will not look quite so bad. You know the old saying:

'Never a road so long is there

But it reaches a turn at last;

Never a cloud that gathers swift But

disappears as fast.'

You think you couldn't possibly feel any worse than you do right now, but you could. Many a time I have had to go hungry longer than this. After we have rested awhile we will go over to the Old Pasture. Perhaps we will have better luck there."

So Reddy tried to forget the emptiness of his stomach and actually had a nap, for he was very, very tired. When he awoke he felt better.

"Well, Granny," said he, "let's start for the Old Pasture. The snow has crusted over, and we won't find it such hard going as it was last night."

Granny arose and followed Reddy out to the doorstep. She walked stiffly. The truth is, she ached in every one of her old bones. At least, that is the way it seemed to her. She looked towards the Old Pasture. It seemed very far away. She sighed wearily. "I don't believe I'll go, Reddy," said she. "You run along and luck go with you."

Reddy turned and stared at Granny suspiciously. You know his is a very suspicious nature. Could it be that Granny had some secret plan of her own to get a meal and wanted to get rid of him?

"What's the matter with you?" he demanded roughly. "It was you who proposed going over to the Old Pasture."

Granny smiled. It was a sad sort of smile. She is wonderfully sharp and smart, is Granny Fox, and she knew what was in Reddy's mind as well as if he had told her.

"Old bones don't rest and recover as quickly as young bones, and I just don't feel equal to going over there now," said she. "The truth is, Reddy, I am growing old. I am going to stay right here and rest. Perhaps then I'll feel able to go hunting to-night. You trot along now, and if you get more than a stomachful, just remember old Granny and bring her a bite."

There was something in the way Granny spoke that told Reddy she was speaking the truth. It was the very first time she ever had admitted that she was growing old and was no longer the equal of any Fox. Never before had he noticed how gray she had grown. Reddy felt a feeling of shame creep over him,—shame that he had suspected Granny of playing a sharp trick. And this little feeling of shame was followed instantly by a splendid thought. He would go out and find food of some kind, and he would bring it straight back to Granny. He had been taken care of by Granny when he was little, and now he would repay Granny for all she had done for him by taking care of her in her old age.

"Go back in the house and lie down, Granny," said he kindly. "I am going to get something, and whatever it may be you shall have your share." With this he trotted off towards the Old Pasture and somehow he didn't mind the ache in his stomach as he had before.

CHAPTER XIV

Three Vain And Foolish Wishes

There's nothing so foolishly silly and vain

As to wish for a thing you can never attain.

—Old Granny Fox.

We all know that, yet most of us are just foolish enough to make such a wish now and then. I guess you have done it. I know I have. Peter Rabbit has done it often and then laughed at himself afterwards. I suspect that even shrewd, clever old Granny Fox has been guilty of it more than once. So it is not surprising that Reddy Fox, terribly hungry as he was, should do a little foolish wishing.

When he left home to go to the Old Pasture, in the hope that he would be able to find something to eat there, he started off bravely. It was cold, very cold indeed, but his fur coat kept him warm as long as he was moving. The Green Meadows were glistening white with snow. All the world, at least all that part of it with which Reddy was acquainted, was white. It was beautiful, very beautiful, as millions of sparkles flashed in the sun. But Reddy had no thought for beauty; the only thought he had room for was to get something to put in the empty stomachs of himself and Granny Fox.

Jack Frost had hardened the snow so that Reddy no longer had to wade through it. He could run on the crust now without breaking through. This made it much easier, so he trotted along swiftly. He had intended to go straight to the Old Pasture, but there suddenly popped into his head a memory of the shelter down in a far corner of the Old Orchard which Farmer Brown's boy had built for Bob White. Probably the Bob White family were there now, and he might surprise them. He would go there first.

Reddy stopped and looked carefully to make sure that Farmer Brown's boy and Bowser the Hound were nowhere in sight. Then he ran swiftly towards the Old Orchard. Just as he entered it he heard a merry voice just over his head: "Dee, dee, dee, dee!" Reddy stopped and looked up. There was Tommy Tit the Chickadee clinging tightly to a big piece of fresh suet tied fast to a branch of a tree, and Tommy was stuffing himself. Reddy sat down right underneath that suet and looked up longingly. The sight of it made his mouth water so that it was almost more than he could stand. He jumped once. He jumped twice. He jumped three times. But all his jumping was in vain. That suet was beyond his reach. There was no possible way of reaching it save by flying or climbing. Reddy's tongue hung out of his mouth with longing.

"I wish I could climb," said Reddy.

But he couldn't climb, and all the wishing in the world wouldn't enable him to, as he very well knew. So after a little he started on. As he drew near the far corner of the Old Orchard, he saw Bob White and Mrs. Bob and all the young Bobs picking up grain which Farmer Brown's boy had scattered for them just in front of the shelter he had built for them. Reddy crouched down and very slowly, an inch at a time, he crept forward, his eyes shining with eagerness. Just as he was almost within springing distance, Bob White gave a signal, and away flew the Bob Whites to the safety of a hemlock-tree on the edge of the Green Forest.

Tears of rage and disappointment welled up in Reddy's eyes. "I wish I could fly," he muttered, as he watched the brown birds disappear in the big hemlock-tree.

This was quite as foolish a wish as the other, so Reddy trotted on and decided to go down past the Smiling Pool. When he got there he found it, as he expected, frozen over. But just where the Laughing Brook joins it there was a little place where there was open water. Billy Mink was on the ice at its edge, and just as Reddy got there Billy dived in. A minute later he climbed out with a fish in his mouth.

"Give me a bite," begged Reddy.

"Catch your own fish," retorted Billy Mink. "I have to work hard enough for what I get as it is."

Reddy was afraid to go out on the ice where Billy was, and so he sat and watched him eat that fine fish. Then Billy dived into the water again and disappeared. Reddy waited a long time, but Billy did not return. "I wish I could dive," gulped Reddy, thinking of the fine fish somewhere under the ice.

And this wish was quite as foolish as the other wishes.

CHAPTER XV: Reddy Fights A Battle

'T is not the foes that are without

But those that are within

That give us battles that we find

The hardest are to win.

—Old Granny Fox

After the last of his three foolish wishes, Reddy Fox left the Smiling Pool and headed straight for the Old Pasture for which he had started in the first place. He wished now that he had gone straight there. Then he wouldn't have seen the suet tied out of reach to the branch of a tree in the Old Orchard; he wouldn't have seen the Bob Whites fly away to safety just as he felt almost sure of catching one; he wouldn't have seen Billy Mink bring a fine fish out of the water and eat it right before him. It is bad enough to be starving with no food in sight, but to be as hungry as Reddy Fox was and to see food just out of reach, to smell it, and not be able to get it is,—well, it is more than most folks can stand patiently.

So Reddy Fox was grumbling to himself as he hurried to the Old Pasture and his heart was very bitter. It seemed to him that everything was against him. His neighbors had food, but he had none, not so much as a crumb. It was unfair. Old Mother Nature was unjust. If he could climb he could get food. If he could fly he could get food. If he could dive he could get food. But he could neither climb, fly, nor dive. He didn't stop to think that Old Mother Nature had given him some of the sharpest wits in all the Green Forest or on all the Green Meadows; that she had given him a wonderful nose; that she had given him the keenest of ears; that she had given him speed excelled by few. He forgot these things and was so busy thinking bitterly of the things he didn't have that he forgot to use his wits and nose and ears when he reached the Old Pasture. The result was that he trotted right past Old

Jed Thumper, the big gray Rabbit, who was sitting behind a little bush holding his breath. The minute Old Jed saw that Reddy was safely past, he started for his bull-briar castle as fast as he could.

It was not until then that Reddy discovered him. Of course, Reddy started after him, and this time he made good use of his speed. But he was too late. Old Jed Thumper reached his castle with Reddy two jumps behind him. Reddy knew now that there was no chance to catch Old Jed that day, and for a few minutes he felt more bitter than ever. Then all in a flash Reddy Fox became the shrewd, clever fellow that he really is. he grinned.

"It's of no use to try to fill an empty stomach on wishes," said he.

"If I had come straight here and minded my own business, I'd have caught old Jed Thumper. Now I'm going to get some food and I'm not going home until I do."

Very wisely Reddy put all unpleasant thoughts out of his head and settled down to using his wits and his eyes and his ears and his nose for all they were worth, as Old Mother Nature had intended he should.

All through the Old Pasture he hunted, taking care not to miss a single place where there was the least chance of finding food. But it was all in vain. Reddy gulped down his disappointment.

"Now for the Big River," said he, and started off bravely.

When he reached the edge of the Big River, he hurried along the bank until he reached a place where the water seldom freezes. As he had hoped, he found that it was not frozen now. It looked so black and cold that it made him shiver just to see it. Back and forth with his nose to the ground he ran. Suddenly he stopped and sniffed. Then he sniffed again. Then he followed his nose straight to the very edge of the Big River. There, floating in the black water, was a dead fish! By wading in he could get it.

Reddy shivered at the touch of the cold water, but what were wet feet compared with such an empty stomach as his? In a minute he had that fish and was back on the shore. It wasn't a very big fish, but it would stop the ache in his stomach until he could get something more. With a sigh of pure happiness he sank his teeth into it and then—well, then he remembered poor Old Granny Fox. Reddy swallowed a mouthful and tried to forget Granny. But he couldn't. He swallowed another mouthful. Poor old Granny was back there at home as hungry as he was and too stiff and tired to hunt. Reddy choked. Then he began a battle with himself. His stomach demanded that fish. If he ate it, no one would be the wiser. But Granny needed it even more than he did. For a long time Reddy fought with himself. In the end he picked up the fish and started for home.

CHAPTER XVI

Reddy Is Made Truly Happy

It's what you do for others,
Not what they do for you,
That makes you feel so happy
All through and through and through.
—Old Granny Fox.

Reddy Fox ran all the way home from the Big River just as fast as he could go. In his mouth he carried the fish he had found and from which he had taken just two bites. You remember he had had a battle with himself over that fish, and now he was running away from himself. That sounds funny, doesn't it? But it was true. Yes, Sir, Reddy Fox was running away from himself. He was afraid that if he didn't get home to Old Granny Fox with that fish very soon, he would eat every last bit of it himself. So he was running his very hardest so as to get there before this could happen. So really he was running away from himself, from his selfish self.

Old Granny Fox was on the doorstep watching for him, and he saw just how her hungry old eyes brightened when she saw him and what he had.

"I've brought you something to eat, Granny," he panted, as he laid the fish at her feet. He was quite out of breath with running. "It isn't much, but it is something. It is all I could find for you."

Granny looked at the fish and then she looked sharply at Reddy, and into those keen yellow eyes of hers crept a soft, tender look, such a look as you would never have believed they could have held.

"What have YOU had to eat?" asked Granny softly.

Reddy turned his head that Granny might not see his face. "Oh, I've had something," said he, trying to speak lightly. It was true; he had had two bites from that fish.

Now you know just how shrewd and smart and wise Granny Fox is. Reddy didn't fool her just the least little bit. She took two small bites from the fish.

"Now," said she, "we'll divide it," and she bit in two parts what remained. In a twinkling she had gulped down the smallest part, for you know she was very, very hungry. "That is your share," said she, as she pushed what remained over to Reddy.

Reddy tried to refuse it. "I brought it all for you," said he. "I know you did, Reddy," replied Granny, and it seemed to Reddy that he never had known her voice to sound so gentle. "You brought it to me when all you had had was the two little bites you had taken from it. You can't fool me, Reddy Fox. There wasn't one good meal for either of us in that fish, but there was enough to give us both a little hope and keep us from starving. Now you mind what I say and eat your share." Granny said this last very sternly.

Reddy looked at Granny, and then he bolted down that little piece of fish without another word.

"That's better," said Granny. "We will feel better, both of us. Now that I've something in my stomach, I feel two years younger. Before you came, I didn't feel as if I should ever be able to go on another hunt. If you hadn't brought something, I—I'm afraid I couldn't have lasted much longer. By another day you probably wouldn't have had old Granny to think of. You may not know it, but I know that you saved my life, Reddy. I had reached a point where I just had to have a little food. You know there are times when a very little food is of more good than a lot of food could be later. This was one of those times."

Never in all his life had Reddy Fox felt so truly happy. He was still hungry,—very, very hungry. But he gave it no thought. He had saved Granny Fox, good old Granny who had taught him all he knew. And he knew that Granny knew how he had had to fight with himself to do it. Reddy was happy through and through with the great happiness that comes from having done something for some one else.

"It was nothing," he muttered.

"It was a very great deal," replied Granny. And then she changed the subject. "How would you like to eat a dinner of Bowser the Hound's?" she asked.

CHAPTER XVII

Granny Fox Promises Reddy Bowser's Dinner

To give her children what each needs
To get the most from life he can,
To work and play and live his best,
Is wise Old Mother Nature's plan.
—Old Granny Fox.

Old Granny Fox asked Reddy how he would like to eat a dinner of Bowser the Hound's, Reddy looked at her sharply to see if she were joking or really meant what she said. Granny looked so sober and so much in earnest that Reddy decided she couldn't be joking, even though it did sound that way.

"I certainly would like it, Granny. Yes, indeed, I certainly would like it," said he. "You—you don't suppose he will give us one, do you?"

Granny chuckled. "No, Reddy," said she. "Bowser isn't so generous as all that, especially to Foxes. He isn't going to give us that dinner; we are going to take it away from him. Yes, Sir, we just naturally are going to take it away from, him."

Reddy didn't for the life of him see how it could be possible to take a dinner away from Bowser the Hound. That seemed to him almost as impossible as it was for him to climb or fly or dive. But he had great faith in Granny's cleverness. He remembered how she had so nearly caught Quacker the Duck. He knew that all the time he had been away trying to find something for them to eat, old Granny Fox had been doing more than just rest her tired old bones. He knew that not for one single minute had her sharp wits been idle. He knew that all that time she had been studying and studying to find some way by which they could get something to eat. So great was his faith in Granny just then that if she had told him she would get him a slice of the moon he would have believed her.

"If you say we can take a dinner away from Bowser the Hound, I suppose we can," said Reddy, "though I don't see how. But if we can, let's do it right away. I'm hungry enough to dare almost anything for the sake of something to put in my stomach. It is so empty that little bit of fish we divided is shaking around as if it were lost. Gracious, I could eat a million fish the size of that one! Have you thought of Fanner Brown's hens, Granny?"

"Of course, Reddy! Of course! What a silly question!" replied Granny. "We may have to come to them yet."

"I wish I was at them right now," interrupted Reddy with a sigh.

"But you know what I have told you," went on Granny. "The surest way of getting into trouble is to steal hens. I'm not feeling quite up to being chased by Bowser the Hound just now, and if we came right home we would give away the secret of where we live and might be smoked out, and that would be the end of us. Besides, those hens will be hard to get this weather, because they will stay in their house, and there is no way for us to get in there unless we walk right in, in broad daylight, and that would never do. It will be a great deal better to take Bowser's dinner away from him. In the first place, if we are careful, no one but Bowser will know about it, and as long as he is chained up, we will have nothing to worry about from him. Besides, we will enjoy getting even with him for the times he has spoiled our chances of catching a fat chicken and for the way he has hunted us. Most decidedly it will be better and safer to try for Bowser's dinner than to try for one of those hens."

"Just as you say, Granny; just as you say," returned Reddy. "You know best. But how under the sun we can do it beats me."

"It is very simple," replied Granny, "very simple indeed. Most things are simple enough when you find out how to do them. Neither of us could do it alone, but together we can do it without the least bit of risk. Listen."

Granny went close to Reddy and whispered to him, although there wasn't a soul within hearing. A slow grin spread over Reddy's face as he listened. When she had finished, he laughed right out.

"Granny, you are a wonder!" he exclaimed admiringly. "I never should have thought of that. Of course we can do it. My, won't Bowser be surprised! And how mad he'll be! Come on, let's be starting!"

"All right," said Granny, and the two started towards Farmer Brown's.

CHAPTER XVIII

Why Bowser The Hound Didn't Eat His Dinner

The thing you've puzzled most about

Is simple once you've found it out.

—Old Granny Fox.

Bowser The Hound dearly loves to hunt just for the pleasure of the chase. It isn't so much the desire to kill as it is the pleasure of using that wonderful nose of his and the excitement of trying to catch some one, especially Granny or Reddy Fox. Farmer Brown's boy had put away his dreadful gun because he no longer wanted to kill the little people of the Green Forest and the Green Meadows, but rather to make them his friends. Bowser had missed the exciting hunts he used to enjoy so much with Farmer Brown's boy. So Bowser had formed the habit of slipping away alone for a hunt every once in a while. When Farmer Brown's boy discovered this, he got a chain and chained Bowser to his little house to keep him from running away and hunting on the sly.

Of course Bowser wasn't kept chained all the time. Oh, my, no! When his master was about, where he could keep an eye on Bowser, he would let him go free. But whenever he was going away and didn't want to take Bowser with him, he would chain Bowser up. Now Bowser always had one good big meal a day. To be sure, he had scraps or a bone now and then besides, but once a day he had one good big meal served to him in a large tin pan. If he happened to be chained, it was brought out to him. If not, it was given to him just outside the kitchen door.

Granny Fox knew all about this. Sly old Granny makes it her business to know the affairs of other people around her because there is no telling when such knowledge may be of use to her. So Granny had watched Bowser the Hound when he and his master had no idea at all that she was anywhere about, and she had found out his ways, the usual hour for his dinner and just how far that chain would allow him to go. It was such things which she had stored away in that shrewd old head of hers that made her so sure she and Reddy could take Bowser's dinner away from him. It was just about Bowser's dinner-time when Granny and Reddy trotted across the snow-covered fields and crept behind the barn until they could peep around the corner. No one was in sight, not even Bowser, who was inside his warm little house at the end of the long shed back of Farmer Brown's house. Granny saw that he was chained and a sly grin crept over her face.

"You stay right here and watch until his dinner is brought out to him," said she to Reddy. "As soon as whoever brings it has gone back to the house you walk right out where Bowser will see you. At the sight of you, he'll forget all about his dinner. Sit right down where he can see you and stay there until you see that I have got that dinner, or until you hear somebody coming, for you know Bowser will make a great racket. Then slip around back of the barn and join me back of that shed."

So Reddy sat down to watch, and Granny left him. By and by Mrs. Brown came out of the house with a pan full of good things. She put it down in front of Bowser's little house and called to him. Then she turned and hurried back, for it was very cold. Bowser came out of his little house, yawned and stretched lazily.

It was time for Reddy to do his part. Out he walked and sat down right in front of Bowser and grinned at him. Bowser stared for a minute as if he doubted his own eyes. Such impudence! Bowser growled. Then with a yelp he sprang towards Reddy.

Now the chain that held him was long, but Reddy had taken care not to get too near, and of course Bowser couldn't reach him. He tugged with all his might and yelped and barked frantically, but Reddy just sat there and grinned in the most provoking manner. It was great fun to tease Bowser this way.

Meanwhile old Granny Fox had stolen out from around the corner of the shed behind Bowser. Getting hold of the edge of the pan with her teeth she pulled it back with her around the corner and out of sight. If she made any noise, Bowser didn't hear it. He was making too much noise himself and was too excited. Presently Reddy heard the sound of an opening door. Mrs. Brown was coming to see what all the fuss was about. Like a flash Reddy darted behind the barn, and all Mrs. Brown saw was Bowser tugging at his chain as he whined and yelped excitedly.

"I guess he must have seen a stray cat or something," said Mrs. Brown and went back in the house. Bowser continued to whine and tug at his chain for a few minutes. Then he gave it up and, growling deep in his throat, turned to eat his dinner. But there wasn't any dinner! It had disappeared, pan and all! Bowser couldn't understand it at all.

Back of the shed Granny and Reddy Fox licked that pan clean; licked it until it was polished. Then, with little sighs of satisfaction, and every once in a while a chuckle, they trotted happily home.

CHAPTER XIX

Old Man Coyote Does A Little Thinking

Investigate and for yourself find out

Those things which most you want to know about.

—Old Granny Fox.

Never in all his life had Reddy Fox enjoyed a dinner more than that one he and Granny had stolen from Bowser the Hound. Of course it would have tasted delicious anyway, because they were so dreadfully hungry, but to Reddy it tasted better still because it had been intended for Bowser. Bowser has hunted Reddy so often that Reddy has no love for him at all, and it tickled him almost to death to think that they had taken his dinner from almost under his nose.

With that good dinner in their stomachs, Reddy and Granny Fox felt so much better that the Great World no longer seemed such a cold and cruel place. Funny how differently things look when your stomach is full from the way those same things look when it is empty. Best of all they knew they could play the same sharp trick again and steal another dinner from Bowser if need be. It is a comforting feeling, a very comforting feeling, to know for a certainty where you can get another meal. It is a feeling that Granny and Reddy Fox and many other little people of the Green Meadows and the Green Forest seldom have in winter. As a rule, when they have eaten one meal, they haven't the least idea where the next one is coming from. How would you like to live that way?

The very next day Granny and Reddy went up to Farmer Brown's at Bowser's dinner hour. But this time Farmer Brown's boy was at work near the barn, and Bowser was not chained. Granny and Reddy stole away as silently as they had come. On the day following they found Bowser chained and stole another dinner from him; then they went away laughing until their sides ached as they heard Bowser's whines of surprise and disappointment when he discovered that his dinner had vanished. They knew by the sound of his voice that he hadn't the least idea what had become of that dinner.

Now there was some one else roaming over the snow-covered meadows and through the Green Forest and the Old Pasture these days with a stomach so lean and empty that he couldn't think of anything else. It was Old Man Coyote. You know he is very clever, is Old Man Coyote, and he managed to find enough food of one kind and another to keep him alive, but never enough to give him that comfortable feeling of a full stomach. While he wasn't actually starving, he was always hungry. So he spent all the time when he wasn't sleeping in hunting for something to eat.

Of course he often ran across the tracks of Granny and Reddy Fox, and once in a while he would meet them. It struck Old Man Coyote that they didn't seem as thin as he was. That set him to thinking. Neither of them was a smarter hunter than he. In fact, he prided himself on being smarter than either of them. Yet when he met them, they seemed to be in the best of spirits and not at all worried because food was so scarce. Why? There must be a reason. They must be getting food of which he knew nothing.

"I'll just keep an eye on them," muttered Old Man Coyote.

So very slyly and cleverly Old Man Coyote followed Granny and Reddy Fox, taking the greatest care that they should not suspect that he was doing it. All one night he followed them through the Green Forest and over the Green Meadows, and when at last he saw them go home, appearing not at all worried because they had caught nothing, he trotted off to his own home to do some more thinking.

"They are getting food somewhere, that is sure," he muttered, as he scratched first one ear and then the other. Somehow he could think better when he was scratching his ears. "If they don't get it in the night, and they certainly didn't get anything this night, they must get it in the daytime. I've done considerable hunting myself in the daytime, and I haven't once met them in the Green Forest or seen them on the Green Meadows or up in the Old Pasture. I wonder if they are stealing Farmer Brown's hens and haven't been found out yet. I've kept away from there myself, but if they can steal hens and not be caught, I certainly can. There never was a Fox yet smart enough to do a thing that a Coyote cannot do if he tries. I think I'll slip up where I can watch Farmer Brown's and see what is going on up there. Yes, Sir, that's what I'll do."

With this, Old Man Coyote grinned and then curled himself up for a short nap, for he was tired.

CHAPTER XX

A Twice Stolen Dinner

No one ever is so smart that some one else

may not prove to be smarter still.

—Old Granny Fox.

Listen and you shall hear all about three rogues. Two were in red and were Granny and Reddy Fox. And one was in gray and was Old Man Coyote. They were the slyest, smartest rogues on all the Green Meadows or in all the Green Forest. All three had started out to steal the same dinner, but the funny part is they didn't intend to steal it from the same person. And still funnier is it that one of them didn't even know where that dinner was or what kind of a dinner it would be.

True to his resolve to know what Granny and Reddy Fox were getting to eat, and where they were getting it, Old Man Coyote hid where he could see what was going on about Farmer Brown's, for it was there he felt sure that Granny and Reddy were getting food. He had waited only a little while when along came Granny and Reddy Fox past the place where Old Man Coyote was hiding. They didn't see him. Of course not. He took care that they should have no chance. But anyway, they were not thinking of him. Their thoughts were all of that dinner they intended to have, and the smart trick by which they would get it.

So with their thoughts all on that dinner they slipped up behind the barn and prepared to work the trick which had been so successful before. Old Man Coyote crept after them. He saw Reddy Fox lie down where he could peep around the corner of the barn to watch Bowser the Hound and to see that no one else was about. He saw Granny leave Reddy there and hurry away. Old Man Coyote's wits worked fast.

"I can't be in two places at once," thought he, "so I can't watch both Granny and Reddy. As I can watch but one, which one shall it be? Granny, of course. Granny is the smartest of the two, and whatever they are up to, she is at the bottom of it. Granny is the one to follow."

So, like a gray shadow, crafty Old Man Coyote stole after Granny Fox and saw her hide behind the corner of the shed at the end of which was the little house of Bowser the Hound. He crept as near as he dared and then lay flat down behind a little bunch of dead grass close to the shed. For some time nothing happened, and Old Man Coyote was puzzled. Every once in a while Granny Fox would look behind and all about to be sure that no danger was near, but she didn't see Old Man Coyote. After what seemed to him a long time, he heard a door open on the other side of the shed. It was Mrs. Brown carrying Bowser's dinner out to him. Of course, Old Man Coyote didn't know this. He knew by the sounds that some one had come out of the house, and it made him nervous. He didn't like being so close to Farmer Brown's house in broad daylight. But he kept his eyes on Granny Fox, and he saw her ears prick up in a way that he knew meant that those sounds were just what she had been waiting for.

"If she isn't afraid, I don't need to be," thought he craftily. After a few minutes he heard a door close and knew that whoever had come out had gone back into the house. Almost at once Bowser the Hound began to yelp and whine. Swiftly Granny Fox disappeared around the corner of the shed. Just as swiftly Old Man Coyote ran forward and peeped around the corner. There was Bowser the Hound tugging at his chain, and just beyond his reach was Reddy Fox, grinning in the most provoking manner. And there was Granny Fox, backing and dragging after her Bowser's dinner. In a flash Old Man Coyote understood the plan, and he almost chuckled aloud at the cleverness of it. Then he hastily backed behind the shed and waited. In a minute Granny Fox appeared, dragging Bowser's dinner. She was so intent on getting that dinner that she almost backed into Old Man Coyote without suspecting that he was anywhere about.

"Thank you, Granny. You needn't bother about it any longer; I'll take it now," growled Old Man Coyote in Granny's ear.

Granny let go of that dinner as if it burned her tongue, and with a frightened little yelp leaped to one side. A minute later Reddy came racing around from behind the barn eager for his share. What he saw was Old Man Coyote bolting down that twice-stolen dinner while Granny Fox fairly danced with rage.

CHAPTER XXI

Granny And Reddy Talk Things Over.

You'll find as on through life you go
The thing you want may prove to be
The very thing you shouldn't have.
Then seeming loss is gain, you see.
—Old Granny Fox.

If ever two folks were mad away through, those two were Granny and Reddy Fox as they watched Old Man Coyote gobble up the dinner they had so cleverly stolen from Bowser the Hound. It was bad enough to lose the dinner, but it was worse to see some one else eat it after they had worked so hard to get it. "Robber!" snarled Granny. Old Man Coyote stopped eating long enough to grin.

"Thief! Sneak! Coward!" snarled Reddy. Once more Old Man Coyote grinned. When that dinner had disappeared down his throat to the last and smallest crumb, he licked his chops and turned to Granny and Reddy.

"I'm very much obliged for that dinner," said he pleasantly, his eyes twinkling with mischief. "It was the best dinner I have had for a long time. Allow me to say that that trick of yours was as smart a trick as ever I have seen. It was quite worthy of a Coyote. You are a very clever old lady, Granny Fox. Now I hear some one coming, and I would suggest that it will be better for all concerned if we are not seen about here."

He darted off behind the barn like a gray streak, and Granny and Reddy followed, for it was true that some one was coming. You see Bowser the Hound had discovered that something was going on around the corner of the shed, and he made such a racket that Mrs. Brown had come out of the house to see what it was all about. By the time she got around there, all she saw was the empty pan which had held Bowser's dinner. She was puzzled. How that pan could be where it was she couldn't understand, and Bowser couldn't tell her, although he tried his very best. She had been puzzled about that pan two or three times before.

Old Man Coyote lost no time in getting back home, for he never felt easy near the home of man in broad daylight. Granny and Reddy Fox went home too, and there was hate in their hearts,—hate for Old Man Coyote. But once they reached home, Old Granny Fox stopped growling, and presently she began to chuckle.

"What are you laughing at?" demanded Reddy.

"At the way Old Man Coyote stole that dinner from us," replied Granny.

"I hate him! He's a sneaking robber!" snapped Reddy.

"Tut, tut, Reddy! Tut, tut!" retorted Granny. "Be fair-minded. We stole that dinner from Bowser the Hound, and Old Man Coyote stole it from us. I guess he is no worse than we are, when you come to think it over. Now is he?"

"I—I—well, I don't suppose he is, when you put it that way," Reddy admitted grudgingly.

"And he was smart, very smart, to outwit two such clever people as we are," continued Granny. "You will have to agree to that."

"Y-e-s," said Reddy slowly. "He was smart enough, but—"

"There isn't any but, Reddy," interrupted Granny. "You know the law of the Green Meadows and the Green Forest. It is everybody for himself, and anything belongs to one who has the wit or the strength to take it. We had the wit to take that dinner from Bowser the Hound, and Old Man Coyote had the wit to take it from us and the strength to keep it. It was all fair enough, and you know there isn't the least use in crying over spilled milk, as the saying is. We simply have got to be smart enough not to let him fool us again. I guess we won't get any more of Bowser's dinners for a while. We've got to think of some other way of filling our stomachs when the hunting is poor. I think if I could have just one of those fat hens of Farmer Brown's, it would put new strength into my old bones. All summer I warned you to keep away from that henyard, but the time has come now when I think we might try for a couple of those hens."

Reddy pricked up his ears at the mention of fat hens. "I think so too," said he. "When shall we try for one?"

"To-morrow morning," replied Granny. "Now don't bother me while I think out a plan."

CHAPTER XXII

Granny Fox Plans To Get A Fat Hen

Full half success for Fox or Man

Is won by working out a plan.

—Old Granny Fox.

Granny Fox knows this. No one knows it better. Whatever she does is first carefully planned in her wise old head. So now after she had decided that she and Reddy would try for one of Farmer Brown's fat hens, she lay down to think out a plan to get that fat hen. No one knew better than she how foolish it would be to go over to that henyard and just trust to luck for a chance to catch one of those biddies. Of course, they might be lucky and get a hen that way, but then again they might be unlucky and get in a peck of trouble.

"You see," said she to Reddy, "we must not only plan how to get that fat hen, but we must also plan how to get away with it safely. If only there was some way of getting in that henhouse at night, there would be no trouble at all. I don't suppose there is the least chance of that."

"Not the least chance in the world," replied Reddy. "There isn't a hole anywhere big enough for even Shadow the Weasel to get through, and Farmer Brown's boy is very careful to lock the door every night."

"There's a little hole that the hens go in and out of during the day, which is big enough for one of us to slip through, I believe," said Granny thoughtfully.

"Sure! But it's always closed at night," snapped Reddy. "Besides, to get to that or the door either, you have got to get inside the henyard, and there's a gate to that which we can't open."

"People are sometimes careless,—even you, Reddy," said Granny.

Reddy squirmed uneasily, for he had been in trouble many times through carelessness. "Well, what of it?" he demanded a wee bit crossly.

"Nothing much, only if that hen-yard gate should happen to be left open, and if Farmer Brown's boy should happen to forget to close that little hole that the hens go through, and if we happened to be around at just that time—"

"Too many ifs to get a dinner with," interrupted Reddy.

"Perhaps," replied Granny mildly, "but I've noticed that it is the one who has an eye open for all the little ifs in life that fares the best. Now I've kept an eye on that henyard, and I've noticed that very often Farmer Brown's boy doesn't close the henyard gate at night. I suppose he thinks that if the henhouse door is locked, the gate doesn't matter. Any one who is careless about one thing, is likely to be careless about another. Sometime he may forget to close that hole. I told you that we would try for one of those hens to-morrow morning, but the more I think about it, the more I think it will be wiser to visit that henhouse a few nights before we run the risk of trying to catch a hen in broad daylight. In fact, I am pretty sure I can make Farmer Brown's boy forget to close that gate."

"How?" demanded Reddy eagerly.

Granny grinned. "I'll try it first and tell you afterwards," said she. "I believe Farmer Brown's boy closes the henhouse up just before jolly, round, red Mr. Sun goes to bed behind the Purple Hills, doesn't he?"

Reddy nodded. Many times from a safe hiding-place he had hungrily watched Farmer Brown's boy shut the biddies up. It was always just before the Black Shadows began to creep out from their hiding-places.

"I thought so," said Granny. The truth is, she KNEW so. There was nothing about that henhouse and what went on there that Granny didn't know quite as well as Reddy. "You stay right here this afternoon until I return. I'll see what I can do."

"Let me go along," begged Reddy.

"No," replied Granny in such a decided tone that Reddy knew it would be of no use to tease. "Sometimes two can do what one cannot do alone, and sometimes one can do what two might spoil. Now we may as well take a nap until it is time for Mr. Sun to go to bed. Just you leave it to your old Granny to take care of the first of those ifs. For the other one we'll have to trust to luck, but you know we are lucky sometimes."

With this Granny curled up for a nap, and having nothing better to do, Reddy followed her example.

CHAPTER XXIII

Farmer Brown's Boy Forgets To Close The Gate

How easy 't is to just forget
Until, alas, it is too late.
The most methodical of folks
Sometimes forget to shut the gate.
—Old Granny Fox.

Farmer Brown's Boy is not usually the forgetful kind. He is pretty good about not forgetting. But Farmer Brown's boy isn't perfect by any means. He does forget sometimes, and he is careless sometimes. He would be a funny kind of boy otherwise. But take it day in and day out, he is pretty thoughtful and careful.

The care of the hens is one of Farmer Brown's boy's duties. It is one of those duties which most of the time is a pleasure. He likes the biddies, and he likes to take care of them. Every morning one of the first things he does is to feed them and open the henhouse so that they can run in the henyard if they want to. Every night he goes out just before dark, collects the eggs and locks the henhouse so that no harm can come to the biddies while they are asleep on their roosts. After the big snowstorm he had shovelled a place in the henyard where the hens could come out and exercise and get a sun-bath when they wanted to, and in the very warmest part of the clay they would do this. Always in the daytime he took the greatest care to see that the henyard gate was fastened, for no one knew better than he how bold Granny and Reddy Fox can be when they are very hungry, and in winter they are very apt to be very hungry most of the time. So he didn't intend to give them a chance to slip into that henyard while the biddies were out, or to give the biddies a chance to stray outside where they might be still more easily caught.

But at night he sometimes left that gate open, as Granny Fox had found out. You see, he thought it didn't matter because the hens were locked in their warm house and so were safe, anyway.

It was just at dusk of the afternoon of the day when Granny and Reddy Fox had talked over a plan to get one of those fat hens that Farmer Brown's boy collected the eggs and saw to it that the biddies had gone to roost for the night. He had just started to close the little sliding door across the hole through which the hens went in and out in the daytime when Bowser the Hound began to make a great racket, as if terribly excited about something.

Farmer Brown's boy gave the little sliding door a hasty push, picked up his basket of eggs, locked the henhouse door and hurried out through the gate without stopping to close it. You see, he was in a hurry to find out what Bowser was making such a fuss about. Bowser was yelping and whining and tugging at his chain, and it was plain to see that he was terribly eager to be set free.

"What is it, Bowser, old boy? Did you see something?" asked Farmer Brown's boy as he patted Bowser on the head. "I can't let you go, you know, because you probably would go off hunting all night and come home in the morning all tired out and with sore feet. Whatever it was, I guess you've scared it out of a year's growth, old fellow, so we'll let it go at that."

Bowser still tugged at his chain and whined, but after a little he quieted down. His master looked around behind the barn to see if he could see what had so stirred up Bowser, but nothing was to be seen, and he returned, patted Bowser once more, and went into the house, never once giving that open henyard gate another thought.

Half an hour later old Granny Fox joined Reddy Fox, who was waiting on the doorstep of their home. "It is all right, Reddy; that gate is open," said she.

"How did you do it, Granny?" asked Reddy eagerly.

"Easily enough," replied Granny. "I let Bowser get a glimpse of me just as his master was locking up the henhouse. Bowser made a great fuss, and of course, Farmer Brown's boy hurried out to see what it was all about. He was in too much of a hurry to close that gate, and afterwards he forgot all about it or else he thought it didn't matter. Of course, I didn't let him get so much as a glimpse of me."

"Of course," said Reddy.

CHAPTER XXIV

A Midnight Visit

By those who win 't is well agreed

He'll try and try who would succeed.

—Old Granny Fox.

It seemed to Reddy Fox as if time never had dragged so slowly as it did this particular night while he and Granny Fox waited until Granny thought it safe to visit Farmer Brown's henhouse and see if by any chance there was a way of getting into it. Reddy tried not to hope too much. Granny had found a way to get the gate to the henyard left open, but this would do them no good unless there was some way of getting into the house, and this he very much doubted. But if there was a way he wanted to know it, and he was impatient to start.

But Granny was in no hurry. Not that she wasn't just as hungry for a fat hen as was Reddy, but she was too wise and clever and altogether too sly to run any risks.

"There is nothing gained by being in too much of a hurry, Reddy," said she, "and often a great deal is lost in that way. A fat hen will taste just as good a little later as it would now, and it will be foolish to go up to Farmer Brown's until we are sure that everybody up there is asleep. But to ease your mind, I'll tell you what we will do; we'll go where we can see Farmer Brown's house and watch until the last light winks out."

So they trotted to a point where they could see Farmer Brown's house, and there they sat down to watch. It seemed to Reddy that those lights never would wink out. But at last they did.

"Come on, Granny!" he cried, jumping to his feet.

"Not yet, Reddy. Not yet," replied Granny. "We've got to give folks time to get sound asleep. If we should get into that henhouse, those hens might make a racket, and if anything like that is going to happen, we want to be sure that Farmer Brown and Farmer Brown's boy are asleep."

This was sound advice, and Reddy knew it. So with a groan he once more threw himself down on the snow to wait. At last Granny arose, stretched, and looked up at the twinkling stars. "Come on," said she and led the way.

Up back of the barn and around it they stole like two shadows and quite as noiselessly as shadows. They heard Bowser the Hound sighing in his sleep in his snug little house, and grinned at each other. Silently they stole over to the henyard. The gate was open, just as Granny had told Reddy it would be. Across the henyard they trotted swiftly, straight to where more than once in the daytime they had seen the hens come out of the house through a little hole. It was closed. Reddy had expected it would be. Still, he was dreadfully disappointed. He gave it merely a glance.

"I knew it wouldn't be any use," said he with a half whine.

But Granny paid no attention to him. She went close to the hole and pushed gently against the little door that closed it. It didn't move. Then she noticed that at one edge there was a tiny crack. She tried to push her nose through, but the crack was too narrow. Then she tried a paw. A claw caught on the edge of the door, and it moved ever so little. Then Granny knew that the little door wasn't fastened. Granny stretched herself flat on the ground and went to work, first with one paw, then with the other. By and by she caught her claws in it just right again, and it moved a wee bit more. No, most certainly that door wasn't fastened, and that crack was a little wider.

"What are you wasting your time there for?" demanded Reddy crossly. "We'd better be off hunting if we would have anything to eat this night."

Granny said nothing but kept on working. She had discovered that this was a sliding door. Presently the crack was wide enough for her to get her nose in. Then she pushed and twisted her head this way and that. The little door slowly slid back, and when Reddy turned to speak to her again, for he had had his back to her, she was nowhere to be seen. Reddy just gaped and gaped foolishly. There was no Granny Fox, but there was a black hole where she had been working, and from it came the most delicious smell,—the smell of fat hens! It seemed to Reddy that his stomach fairly flopped over with longing. He rubbed his eyes to be sure that he was awake. Then in a twinkling he was inside that hole himself.

"Sh-h-h, be still!" whispered Old Granny Fox.

CHAPTER XXV

A Dinner For Two

Dark deeds are done in the stilly night,

And who shall say if they're wrong or right?

—Old Granny Fox.

It all depends on how you look at things. Of course, Granny and Reddy Fox had no business to be in Farmer Brown's henhouse in the middle of the night, or at any other time, for that matter. That is, they had no business to be there, as Farmer Brown would look at the matter. He would have called them two red thieves. Perhaps that is just what they were. But looking at the matter as they did, I am not so sure about it. To Granny and Reddy Fox those hens were simply big, rather stupid birds, splendid eating if they could be caught, and bound to be eaten by somebody. The fact that they were in Farmer Brown's henhouse didn't make them his any more than the fact that Mrs. Grouse was in a part of the Green Forest owned by Farmer Brown made her his.

You see, among the little meadow and forest people there is no such thing as property rights, excepting in the matter of storehouses, and because these hens were alive, it didn't occur to Granny and Reddy that the henhouse was a sort of storehouse. It would have made no difference if it had. Among the little people it is considered quite right to help yourself from another's storehouse if you are smart enough to find it and really need the food.

Besides, Reddy and Granny knew that Fanner Brown and his boy would eat some of those hens themselves, and they didn't begin to need them as Reddy and Granny did. So as they looked at the matter, there was nothing wrong in being in that henhouse in the middle of the night. They were there simply because they needed food very, very much, and food was there.

They stared up at the roosts where the biddies were huddled together, fast asleep. They were too high up to be reached from the floor even when Reddy and Granny stood on their hind legs and stretched as far as they could.

"We've got to wake them up and scare them so that some of the silly things will fly down where we can catch them," said Reddy, licking his lips hungrily.

"That won't do at all!" snapped Granny. "They would make a great racket and waken Bowser the Hound, and he would waken his master, and that is just what we mustn't do if we hope to ever get in here again. I thought you had more sense, Reddy."

Reddy looked a little shamefaced. "Well, if we don't do that, how are we going to get them? We can't fly," he grumbled.

"You stay right here where you are," snapped Granny, "and take care that you don't make a sound."

Then Granny jumped lightly to a little shelf that ran along in front of the nesting boxes. From this she could reach the lower roost on which four fat hens were asleep. Very gently she pushed her head in between two of these and crowded them apart. Sleepily they protested and moved along a little. Granny continued to crowd them. At last one of them stretched out her head to see who was crowding so. Like a flash Granny seized that head, and biddy never knew what had wakened her, nor did she have a chance to waken the others.

Dropping this hen at Reddy's feet, Granny crowded another until she did the same thing, and just the same thing happened once more. Then Granny jumped lightly down, picked up one of the hens by the neck, slung the body over her shoulder, and told Reddy to do the same with the other and start for home.

"Aren't you going to get any more while we have the chance?" grumbled Reddy.

"Enough is enough," retorted Granny. "We've got a dinner for two, and so far no one is any the wiser. Perhaps these two won't be missed, and we'll have a chance to get some more another night. Now come on."

This was plain common sense, and Reddy knew it, so without another word he followed old Granny Fox out by the way they had entered, and then home to the best dinner he had had for a long long time.

CHAPTER XXVI

Farmer Brown's Boy Sets A Trap

The trouble is that troubles are,
More frequently than not,
Brought on by naught but carelessness;
By some one who forgot.
—Old Granny Fox.

Granny Fox had hoped that those two hens she and Reddy had stolen from Farmer Brown's henhouse would not be missed, but they were. They were missed the very first thing the next morning when Farmer Brown's boy went to feed the biddies. He discovered right away that the little sliding door which should have closed the opening through which the hens went in and out of the house was open, and then he remembered that he had left the henyard gate open the night before. Carefully Farmer Brown's boy examined the hole with the sliding door.

"Ha!" said he presently, and held up two red hairs which he had found on the edge of the door. "Ha! I thought as much. I was careless last night and didn't fasten this door, and I left the gate open. Reddy Fox has been here, and now I know what has become of those two hens. I suppose it serves me right for my carelessness, and I suppose if the truth were known, those hens were of more real good to him than they ever could have been to me, because the poor fellow must be having pretty hard work to get a living these hard winter days. Still, I can't have him stealing any more. That would never do at all. If I shut them up every night and am not careless, he can't get them. But accidents will happen, and I might do just as I did last night—think I had locked up when I hadn't. I don't like to set a trap for Reddy, but I must teach the rascal a lesson. If I don't, he will get so bold that those chickens won't be safe even in broad daylight."

Now at just that very time over in their home, Granny and Reddy Fox were talking over plans for the future, and shrewd old Granny was pointing out to Reddy how necessary it was that they should keep away from that henyard for some time. "We've had a good dinner, a splendid dinner, and if we are smart enough we may be able to get more good dinners where this one came from," said she. "But we certainly won't if we are too greedy."

"But I don't believe Farmer Brown's boy has missed those two chickens, and I don't see any reason at all why we shouldn't go back there to-night and get two more if he is stupid enough to leave that gate and little door open," whined Reddy.

"Maybe he hasn't missed those two, but if we should take two more he certainly would miss them, and he would guess what had become of them, and that might get us into no end of trouble," snapped Granny. "We are not starving now, and the best thing for us to do is to keep away from that henhouse until we can't get anything to eat anywhere else, Now you mind what I tell you, Reddy, and don't you dare go near there."

Reddy promised, and so it came about that Farmer Brown's boy hunted up a trap all for nothing so far as Reddy and Granny were concerned. Very carefully he bound strips of cloth around the jaws of the trap, for he couldn't bear to think of those cruel jaws cutting into the leg of Reddy, should he happen to get caught. You see, Farmer Brown's boy didn't intend to kill Reddy if he should catch him, but to make him a prisoner for a while and so keep him out of mischief. That night he hid the trap very cunningly just inside the henhouse where any one creeping through that little hole made for the hens to go in and out would be sure to step in it. Then he purposely left the little sliding door open part way as if it had been forgotten, and he also left the henyard gate open just as he had done the night before.

"There now, Master Reddy," said he, talking to himself, "I rather think that you are going to get into trouble before morning."

And doubtless Reddy would have done just that thing but for the wisdom of sly old Granny.

CHAPTER XXVII

Prickly Porky Takes A Sun Bath

Danger comes when least expected;

'T is often near when not expected.

—Old Granny Fox.

The long hard winter had passed, and Spring had come. Prickly Porky the Porcupine came down from a tall poplar-tree and slowly stretched himself. He was tired of eating. He was tired of swinging in the tree-top.

"I believe I'll have a sun-bath," said Prickly Porky, and lazily walked toward the edge of the Green Forest in search of a place where the sun lay warm and bright.

Now Prickly Porky's stomach was very, very full. He was fat and naturally lazy, so when he came to the doorstep of an old house just on the edge of the Green Forest he sat down to rest. It was sunny and warm there, and the longer he sat the less like moving he felt. He looked about him with his dull eyes and grunted to himself.

"It's a deserted house. Nobody lives here, and I guess nobody'll care if I take a nap right here on the doorstep," said Prickly Porky to himself. "And I don't care if they do," he added, for Prickly Porky the Porcupine was afraid of nobody and nothing.

So Prickly Porky made himself as comfortable as possible, yawned once or twice, tried to wink at jolly, round, red Mr. Sun, who was winking and smiling down at him and then fell fast asleep right on the doorstep of the old house.

Now the old house had been deserted. No one had lived in it for a long, long time, a very long time indeed. But it happened that, the night before, old Granny Fox and Reddy Fox had had to move out of their nice home on the edge of the Green Meadows because Farmer Brown's boy had found it. Reddy was very stiff and sore, for he had been shot by a hunter. He was so sore he could hardly walk, and could not go very far. So old Granny Fox had led him to the old deserted house and put him to bed in that.

"No one will think of looking for us here, for every one knows that no one lives here," said old Granny Fox, as she made Reddy as comfortable as possible.

As soon as it was daylight, Granny Fox slipped out to watch for Farmer Brown's boy, for she felt sure that he would come back to the house they had left, and sure enough he did. He brought a spade and dug the house open, and all the time old Granny Fox was watching him from behind a fence corner and laughing to think that she had been smart enough to move in the night.

But Reddy Fox didn't know anything about this. He was so tired that he slept and slept and slept. It was the middle of the morning when finally he awoke. He yawned and stretched, and when he stretched he groaned because he was so stiff and sore. Then he hobbled up toward the doorway to see if old Granny Fox had left any breakfast outside for him.

It was dark, very dark. Reddy was puzzled. Could it be that he had gotten up before daylight—that he hadn't slept as long as he thought? Perhaps he had slept the whole day through, and it was night again. My, how hungry he was!

"I hope Granny has caught a fine, fat chicken for me," thought Reddy, and his mouth watered.

Just then he ran bump into something. "Wow!" screamed Reddy Fox, and clapped both hands to his nose. Something was sticking into it. It was one of the sharp little spears that Prickly Porky hides in his coat. Reddy Fox knew then why the old house was so dark. Prickly Porky was blocking up the doorway.

CHAPTER XXVIII

Prickly Porky Enjoys Himself

A boasting tongue, as sure as fate,

Will trip its owner soon or late.

—Old Granny Fox.

Prickly Porky the Porcupine was enjoying himself. There was no doubt about that. He was stretched across the doorway of that old house, the very house in which old Granny Fox had been born. When he had lain down on the doorstep for a nap and sun-bath, he had thought that the old house was still deserted. Then he had fallen asleep, only to be wakened by Reddy Fox, who bad been asleep in the old house and who couldn't get out because Prickly Porky was in the way.

Now Prickly Porky does not love Reddy Fox, and the more Reddy begged and scolded and called him names, the more Prickly Porky chuckled. It was such a good joke to think that he had trapped Reddy Fox, and he made up his mind that he would keep Reddy in there a long time just to tease him and make him uncomfortable. You see Prickly Porky remembered how often Reddy Fox played mean tricks on little meadow and forest folks who are smaller and weaker than himself.

"It will do him good. It certainly will do him good," said Prickly Porky, and rattled the thousand little spears hidden in his long coat, for he knew that the very sound of them would make Reddy Fox shiver with fright.

Suddenly Prickly Porky pricked up his funny little short ears. He heard the deep voice of Bowser the Hound, and it was coming nearer and nearer. Prickly Porky chuckled again.

"I guess Mr. Bowser is going to have a surprise; I certainly think he is," said Prickly Porky as he made all the thousand little spears stand out from his long coat till he looked like a funny great chestnut burr.

Bowser the Hound did have a surprise. He was hunting Reddy Fox, and he almost ran into Prickly Porky before he saw him. The very sight of those thousand little spears sent little cold chills chasing each other down Bowser's backbone clear to the tip of his tail, for he remembered how he had gotten some of them in his lips and mouth once upon a time, and how it had hurt to have them pulled out. Ever since then he had had the greatest respect for Prickly Porky.

"Wow!" yelped Bowser the Hound, stopping short. "I beg your pardon, Prickly Porky, I beg your pardon, I didn't know you were taking a nap here."

All the time Bowser the Hound was backing away as fast as he could. Then he turned around, put his tail between his legs and actually ran away.

Slowly Prickly Porky unrolled, and his little eyes twinkled as he watched Bowser the Hound run away.

"Bowser's very big and strong;
His voice is deep; his legs are long;
His bark scares some almost to death.
But as for me he wastes his breath;
I just roll up and shake my spears
And Bowser is the one who fears."

So said Prickly Porky, and laughed aloud. Just then he heard a light footstep and turned to see who was coming. It was old Granny Fox. She had seen Bowser run away, and now she was anxious to find out if Reddy Fox were safe.

"Good morning," said Granny Fox, taking care not to come too near.

"Good morning," replied Prickly Porky, hiding a smile.

"I'm very tired and would like to go inside my house; had you just as soon move?" asked Granny Fox.

"Oh!" exclaimed Prickly Porky, "is this your house? I thought you lived over on the Green Meadows."

"I did, but I've moved. Please let me in," replied Granny Fox.

"Certainly, certainly. Don't mind me, Granny Fox. Step right over me," said Prickly Porky, and smiled once more, and at the same time rattled his little spears.

Instead of stepping over him, Granny Fox backed away.

CHAPTER XXIX

The New Home In The Old Pasture

Who keeps a watch upon his toes
Need never fear he'll bump his nose.
—Old Granny Fox.

Now there is nothing like being shut in alone in the dark to make one think. A voice inside of Reddy began to whisper to him. "If you hadn't tried to be smart and show off you wouldn't have brought all this trouble on yourself and Old Granny Fox," said the voice.

"I know it," replied Reddy right out loud, forgetting that it was only a small voice inside of him.

"What do you know?" asked Prickly Porky. He was still keeping Reddy in and Granny out and he had overheard what Reddy said.

"It is none of your business!" snapped Reddy.

Reddy could hear Prickly Porky chuckle. Then Prickly Porky repeated as if to himself in a queer cracked voice the following:

"Rudeness never, never pays,
Nor is there gain in saucy ways.
It's always best to be polite
And ne'er give way to ugly spite.
If that's the way you feel inside
You'd better all such feelings hide;
For he must smile who hopes to win,
And he who loses best will grin."

Reddy pretended that he hadn't heard. Prickly Porky continued to chuckle for a while and finally Reddy fell asleep. When he awoke it was to find that Prickly Porky had left and old Granny Fox had brought him something to eat.

Just as soon as Reddy Fox was able to travel he and Granny had moved to the Old Pasture. The Old Pasture is very different from the Green Meadows or the Green Forest. Yes, indeed, it is very, very different. Reddy Fox thought so. And Reddy didn't like the change,—not a bit. All about were great rocks, and around and over them grew bushes and young trees and bull-briars with long ugly thorns, and blackberry and raspberry canes that seemed to have a million little hooked hands, reaching to catch in and tear his red coat and to scratch his face and hands. There were little open places where wild-eyed young cattle fed on the short grass. They had made many little paths all crisscross among the bushes, and when you tried to follow one of these paths you never could tell where you were coming out.

No, Reddy Fox did not like the Old Pasture at all. There was no long, soft green grass to lie down in. And it was lonesome up there. He missed the little people of the Green Meadows and the Green Forest. There was no one to bully and tease. And it was such a long, long way from Farmer Brown's henyard that old Granny Fox wouldn't even try to bring him a fat hen. At least, that's what she told Reddy.

The truth is, wise old Granny Fox knew that the very best thing she could do was to stay away from Farmer Brown's for a long time. She knew that Reddy couldn't go down there, because he was still too lame and sore to travel such a long way, and she hoped that by the time Reddy was well enough to go, he would have learned better than to do such a foolish thing as to try to show off by stealing a chicken in broad daylight, as he had when he brought all this trouble on them.

Down on the Green Meadows, the home of Granny and Reddy Fox had been on a little knoll, which you know is a little low hill, right where they could sit on their doorstep and look all over the Green Meadows. It had been very, very beautiful down there. They had made lovely little paths through the tall green meadow grass, and the buttercups and daisies had grown close up to their very doorstep. But up here in the Old Pasture Granny Fox had chosen the thickest clump of bushes and young trees she could find, and in the middle was a great pile of rocks. Way in among these rocks Granny Fox had dug their new house. It was right down under the rocks. Even in the middle of the day jolly, round, red Mr. Sun could hardly find it with a few of his long, bright beams. All the rest of the time it was dark and gloomy there.

No, Reddy Fox didn't like his new home at all, but when he said so old Granny Fox boxed his ears.

"It's your own fault that we've got to live here now," said she. "It's the only place where we are safe. Farmer Brown's boy never will find this home, and even if he did he couldn't dig into it as he did into our old home on the Green Meadows. Here we are, and here we've got to stay, all because a foolish little Fox thought himself smarter than anybody else and tried to show off."

Reddy hung his head. "I don't care!" he said, which was very, very foolish, because, you know, he did care a very great deal.

And here we will leave wise Old Granny Fox and Reddy, safe, even if they do not like their new home. You see, Lightfoot the Deer is getting jealous. He thinks there should be some books about the people of the Green Forest, and that the first one should be about him. And because we all love Lightfoot the Deer, the very next book is to bear his name.

❑❑❑